To Chris

Peace

LoVE

HAppiness

Kev

X

TRANSMIGRATIONS

K.R. Stewart

MINERVA PRESS
MONTREUX LONDON WASHINGTON

TRANSMIGRATIONS
Copyright © K.R. Stewart 1995

ISBN 1 85863 435 0

First Published 1995 by
MINERVA PRESS
1 Cromwell Place,
London SW7 2JE

Printed in Great Britain by
B.W.D. Ltd., Northolt, Middlesex.

TRANSMIGRATIONS

ABOUT THE AUTHOR

Kevin Stewart is twenty nine years old.   He was born in Elgin, Scotland, and now lives in Bristol.

Kashmir Nights

The wolves howled madly, the stars shone bright
The distant gun fire in the Kashmir night
The people smile and say hello
Oblivious of their plight
But in the darkness of curfew, they're all locked up in fright
The wolves they howl, the barking dogs, tearing up their prey
Kashmir nights so dark and cold, wishing for the day
The birds sang songs, the mist is rising
The tranquil days of realising
The hawk swoons down the lily lakes
So much to give, but we won't take
The wolves howled madly, the moon shone bright
So peaceful in the Kashmir night.

A Glimmer of Dawn

Zara, Zara, bright as dawn
I see you on the fresh cut lawn
Flourishing with the summer blooms
Please won't you come up to my room?
Zara Zara, I rejoice
Every time I hear your voice
You look so innocent in flowers and stripes
I've got something you will like.
Zara, Zara like the sun
You could have just anyone
I'm the one, you will see
Hate me now but you'll love me.
Zara, Zara don't be alarmed
I won't do you any harm
Stay with me down on the farm
You fill my ego with your charm.
Zara, Zara, bring me joy
There is no need to act so coy
Please don't tell your next of kin
Stay with me through thick and thin.
Zara, Zara, bright as dawn
I saw you smiling but now you've gone.

Judgement Day

Feed me like a little child, I'll snuggle up to you.
Stroke my hair, kiss my head, protect me from those blues
The sky is filled with April showers, will the sun break through?
My mind's made up I'm so stubborn but you're the same way too
Walking through the lonely forest I sit down for my rest -
I close my eyes and dream away of fairies and green elves.
I awoke feeling confused, I'm lying in my bed
My boots are muddy, my clothes have leaves, maybe this time I'm
dead.
Talk to me with honesty for I won't tell a soul
I will reassure your fears for me, the bell has tolled
Take me now with welcome arms for I am fading fast
Give me one kiss my beautiful for this could be my last
Feed me on your milk filled breast to give me back my strength
I am only still but young but I have gone the length.
Deprivation all around, the children cry for food
Where did I go wrong my Lord? All my life I've been so good!
Walking to your house last night a light came from the sky
An angelic figure spoke to me saying it was time to die
My head was spinning with her words, I just could not believe
I begged for mercy at her feet asking for a reprieve
So take me one last lingering time before I say farewell
For this is the last time we shall meet, for you are going to Hell.

A Thousand Swallows

A thousand swallows swooned down on the lake
I was alone in the October night, I'd taken all I could take;
But then the red sky appeared to save
The boats approached to take their slave
A thousand swallows let out a scream
Things are never what they seem
Their teeth shone on the ninth full moon
Judgement day is coming soon
A thousand swallows hid in the dark
The cats they screeched, the dogs they barked.
It was all so beautiful
We danced on fire to fight the chill
A thousand swallows, a million days
Rowing through the Autumn haze.

Satanic Lady

The days were young and full of grace
A haunting smile across her face
I shall devour your very soul
And put you back in to the hole
The days were cold, wrapped up three times
Outside in darkness the church bells chime
Her nails like knives tear at my back
She screams her ecstasy one more attack
The blood drips slowly on the white sheet
Never again will I make the cheat
The days were young but oh so tired
Her eyes go red, she breathes with fire
The days they end no more, the cheer,
She turns her head for one more leer.

The Goddess Of Truth

Glowing like a Goddess, heads turning when you walk
A beauty made in heaven, but your heart is locked
Radiating light, as you glide across the room
Wishing for your soul to mean, my love it will be soon.
Men shower you with diamonds and promise of grandeur
But you're still lost in childhood, dreams not knowing who you are
Searching for the perfect partner, who will hold you when you're frail
A man who will guard your every move, and won't go off the rails.
Take my hand, unfortunate child, I am your heaven sent
All those people who hurt you, it wasn't really meant
I will take you to your wildest dreams and countries far afield
With a kiss, then to my knees, a ring, and our loves sealed.
You amaze me with your smile that could open a thousand doors
But you know just what you want, for that I do adore
I'll walk the highest mountains, I'll swim the treacherous seas
I will fulfil your every wish if you say it's me.
Because you have such beauty, it's made you vain and sad
You can't even smile or sing, but my you're not going mad
You are the Goddess of truth and light, you are the sun's own ray
You are the spring and summer time, so please don't go away.

Rolling Over You

You look so lovely with the morning sun, shining in your face
My knees, they tremble, when I see you dressed up in silks and lace
Won't you come into my world, I want to feel your brain
You are so different from the others, you wouldn't cause me pain
Your beauty astounds me, wondrous and pure, please give me your
soul
I've never met another like you, they're all so dull, so droll;
You look lovely with the moonlight shining on your hair
Take me to your thoughts and fears, I'll make you feel so fair.
You look lovely in my bed, lying next to me
I was blinded by your charm, one kiss, now I can see.

The Kiss of Death

Fulfilling a poor heart, that's had all the blood sucked out
Through suspecting eyes, of the demons that lurk
In a world full of lies, envy and deceit
Her smile's self containing, as he begs at her feet.
Prevailing her innocence, on a speechless smooth face
Her cherry red lips, with the sweetest of taste
She falls in his arms, but the emptiness stays
She was his rainbow, she was his ray.
Now an ocean of memories, flood back in his glass
Another mind eraser, and the pain will pass
Her presence still haunting, throughout every room
There is no light, through the tunnel of doom
Hand in hand with another, the bitterness bites
His body is shaking wishing for the night
In an alcohol daze, he begs her forgiveness
But the emptiness stays, with the taste of her kiss.

The Seasons of Pain

The sun beats down upon her naked brain
She's riddled with remorse, can't shed the blame
For sixteen long days, she's cried an ocean of tears
Her hands shake for comfort, but there's nobody near
All the flowers have died in the winter of doom
She looks for a future, but all she sees is gloom
No will to go on, pulls her tangled hair
She looks like a witch, but who really cares?
Her eye lids half shut, round about they are black
Her spleen's twisted and torn, from the knife in her back
The greatest being she's met, has left in the night
She thought it was righteous, she thought he was right
The rain pours on down, the thunder roars from the sky
They may as well take me, for inside I've died
The lightning strikes with Satanic light
I've nothing to live for, Lord take me tonight
The snow falls down slowly, freezing her blue
She's lost the one creature, that she thought true
The robin gets red singing melodious tunes
I can't stand the pain, please take me soon
The sun beats upon her naked brain
The burden now lifted, she's unlocked the chains
The bluebells and tulips, the air sweet with new life
A new age has dawned, no more the strife.

Deep Down

Deep down in my heart, where once was a fire
A smouldering passion, of forbidden desires
Her Astral white light, makes me feel alive
Unaware of the problems, still to arrive
A mutual chemistry between minds
Like the wind and the sea, so treacherous and wild
Although she's much older, I can see the child
She walks with an elegance, so mellow, so mild
The cigarette burns, right down to your brain
Sending strange signals, that seem so insane
I feel I should ask her, her feelings and thoughts
A fear of rejection, for my soul will rot
Deep down inside, right to the nerve ends
Confused by her eyes, and the message they send
I love this woman, like I never could
But I'm still left alone, like a child in the woods.

Complete

The rain drips from my screaming soul, one smile, my heart is healed
The sky is grey, my heart is blue, please take me to the fields
Hand in Hand we'll walk for miles, the sun beats on our heads
Today's the day my life's complete, yesterday felt dead
You lift my spirit, you know it's right that we should be together
I'll spend my next three lives with you, pain I'll cause you never
The sun beams down upon my face
No more shall I feel cold
You make me feel as if newborn, no more will I be old
I thank you for the joy you bring, our love will never die
You make me laugh, you make me real, you make me feel so high.

Life's Mountains

A vibrant orange as the sun rises in the east of life's mountains, full of surprises
The starlings sing love songs the squirrels they smile
A world full of joy, at the birth of a child
The mist slowly lifts above pearly dew grass
Reaching new spirit, never surpassed
The logs on the fire, give off a red glow
Warming my cheeks, then you say hello
The taste of springtime, enlightens your stride
High in the mountains, where paradise hides
There are no gods to worship or pray
There is no tomorrow, we live for today
The fresh water streams, running down to life's river
I thank you my girl, for the love you deliver
Now we have a boy, very soon he's a man
We have no possessions, but we'll do what we can
When I see your face glowing, my heart fills with pride
I have no enemies now, you're by my side
To the mountains we'll dwell, eat the herbs and the plants
I'll never feel lonely, when you're here to enchant
The moon shines upon us, guiding light through the trees
Your hand in mine, as we walk to the sea
Sitting down on the rocks, listening to the strange sounds
Your arm's wrapped around me forever we're bound
A deepening pink, as the sun rises
In the east of life's mountains, where no one despises.

Back from the Cold

I light a candle for the love that's gone
Inside my head, still hear her song
A million tears come from my eyes -
The jealousy, the small white lies
In my bed, I feel her presence
In my soul her very essence
The lonely nights, stare at the wall
Is she laughing at my fall?

I light a fire, but still it's cold
My face looks young, but I feel old
I look above, seeing the same stars
I wish I knew, just where you are.

I light a candle, all in vain
I never thought, you'd be the same
But it's all right, my spirit's strong
Inside my head, can't hear the song.

Next

Cover me with kisses darling, let me be the one.
Wrap your lovely body round me, you are bringing back the sun.
Hand in hand we walk the miles, in the countryside.
Tell me all your hopes and fears, in me you can confide.
Smother me with love sweet darling, every day's the summertime.
There have been so many to pass, but none with the right sign.
You make me feel so warm, so free, you make me feel so whole;
You touch the very heart of me, you heal my aching soul;
So wrap your spirit round my brain, you've made me see the light.
For so long, my world eclipsed, now you are the star bright.

Armageddon

I look out my window, the rain falls down
Armageddon's drawing near.
The tears run slowly down my cheeks, my heart it fills with fear
Lying on top of my soft double bed, my hand reaches over to touch
On our last hour, I wanted to tell you, I love you ever so much.
Reaching for the whisky bottle, waiting for the fire
My head feels dizzy, my soul is empty, it's you I do desire
It's been so long since you said farewell, and run away with another
I thought that I'd find someone new, but still I've not recovered
A panic button strikes my brain, just half an hour to go
The world will end, then the long winter and you won't even know
I look out of my window, the black rain falls, we hear the doomsday
bell
But all not lost for you and me; our love will blossom in hell.

The Rebirth

Let your love flow through my veins
Kiss my lips erase the pain
Take my hand, for I am yours
Fill my life with love so pure
Take my body I declare
I'll make you feel so free, so fair
Have my soul, the air I breathe
I'll never give you cause to leave.
I love your eyes so alive,
I love your hair, I want your thighs
You make me feel, like ten feet tall
Help me please, don't let me fall.
Walk with me to far-off lands
I'll help you through when you can't stand
I'll mop the fever from your brow
Don't think ahead, for this is now;
So let my love flow through your veins,
The sun has come
There's no more pain.

Soul Sister

Heal me with your spirit dear
Fill my soul, erase my fears
For us meeting must be fate
You're spoken for, is it too late
The warmth that oozes from your smile
Those clear blue eyes, that of a child
You touch me with your spirit clear,
How I wish that you were here!
Tell me everything about your life
Lift the barriers, tell of the strife
Of how you were, before the light
Tell me please it is all right
Fill my heart with love and joy
Lift my mask, you'll find the boy
Come with me, watch the sun set
I'm so glad, that we have met.

Forbidden Fruit

You are my dream, I saw her today
This numbness inside, it won't go away
Our eyes met, a gaze
Does she feel the same?
Can't get through this maze, I'm going insane.
She made me feel wanted
But she's wearing a ring
I won't be taunted, to dance and to sing
I hope I see you, on some far off day
Your smile will meet mine
And it will be our day.
I thank you sweet darling for the feelings you give
No more heading down, for you've made me live.

Sundown

The Summer's gone, the song's been sung
Life has ended, when it should have begun
No peaceful feeling, in the morning sun
She is so happy, now that she has won.
The feeling has gone, I should have guessed
Our life in a muddle, my head in a mess
She pretends she's happy in her new love nest
But one day she'll realise, she lost the best.
My life's now empty, there is now sound
My head is spinning, around and around
Inside, the howling of a thousand hounds -
The winter is here, my heart fills with fear
You think I don't care, but I loved you dear.

Fear

I'll love you tonight, then leave you tomorrow.
There will be no remorse, there's no room for sorrow.
I'd hold you forever, but my heart is hollow.
We'll never know what was to follow.
Kiss me tonight, then say goodbye
When the morning sun touches the sky.
I'm so sorry to lower your high,
But my dear, it's time to fly.
Take me tonight, whatever's your name.
Can't you see I'm playing a game?
Please don't cry, it's such a shame!
It's not your fault, I am to blame.
Come over here and sit by me.
I'd give you my heart, but she's stolen the key;
That's just the way, it has to be.
I'm shaking with fear, why can't you see?
Be with me tonight, and evermore.
My body is empty, my head is sore.
Take me by the hand, open the door.
Please make me happy, for I am so bored.
I'll love you tonight, then say "Farewell".
Satan is awaiting, to take me to hell.
In my mind, there sounds a bell
I have gone crazy, but who can tell?

Stay Forever

My bags are packed, my rambling boots, to travel the world wide.
All it needs is just one word, and I'll stay right by your side.
When you're near, the warmth I feel, the chemistry's unreal.
Won't you lift your barriers, and tell me how you feel?
Do you want me, like I want you? To me you're my soul mate.
I think you feel the same way too.
Please open up the gate.
I have seen the seven wonders, I've sailed the seven seas.
But I'm so lonely without you, just tell me you want me.
It's time to leave, my heart is dead, tell me that I should stay.
I need your love, like nothing else.
I don't want to go away.

Always Yours

You know that I still love you girl, please, you must believe,
But the four winds are calling me, it's time to take my leave.
I need to be alone sometimes, or I'd turn into a bore.
If I stayed, we'd only fight, then leave each other sore.
You know, I'll always care for you, I have to see you smile.
You are the only one I've loved, but I must walk the miles.
I love to watch the sun come up on a lonely beach,
I'll think of you in far off lands, I'm never too far to reach.
If you need a friend to talk, or just someone to cry,
Think of me with smile on face, for I could never lie.
Farewell girl, it's time to go, I'll see you in the next life.
Forgive me please, for it is right, now we are free from strife.

The Four Seasons

As we walked through the fields
Our hearts filled with joy.
My heart, beating faster, as if still a boy.
A new age has dawned, the stars fill my soul.
When you kiss my lips, the tears start to roll.
As we walk by the seaside, the waves are alive.
For so long I've waited, for love to arrive.
I've searched this strange land, I've followed the moon.
I've knocked on the doors, but there was no room.
As the leaves from the trees fall to the ground.
I give you my warmth, now you are safe and sound.
No one can touch us in our sanctuary,
You look in my eyes, but you don't need to say.

Peace

Peace on your soul, love in your life,
I'm the one, lady, to save you from strife.
Success in your world, the sweetest girl,
With your silky touch, I'm in a whirl.
Freedom on you, no need for ties,
In seventy years we shall all die.
Smell the air that we breath, drink the water so pure,
Take my aching heart, for mine is yours.
Love in your soul, the day so mellow,
If you're black or white, if you're red or yellow.
You are the sweetest, I've ever seen.
I know where you're going, I don't care where you've been.
So take my soul, please take my heart.
This world is so hard, let's make a new start.
Love on you girl, forever, and ever.
If you stay with me, we'll never be severed.

June

Your hands touched the book, you gave as a present
I hold it and cherish, for the love it was sent
From heaven you are, feel the tinglings of love
There must be a god, so high up above
At one with myself, I want to cry
When you're near, I can't express, this feeling so high
I thank you my darling, for just being you
The lights had gone out, but it's nothing new
Your innocence shines through with a flash of a smile
The world is so lovely, when you feel like a child
Nothing brings us down, together we make
A life made for sharing, no word such as take
I feel so alive, run my fingers through your hair
So shining, so soft, so precious, so fair
You are the one thing I can't love too much
I'll keep you from dangers, that are sure to lurk
Nothing is sacred, like the madness we share
Nothing will come between, to destroy or tear
I wish I could be with you, for the rest of our lives
The terror of loneliness with the rope and the knife
I need the courage to be your fool
The word's in my brain, but the mouth just drools
I've been so long in darkness but you shone your light
You are so special, you are so right.

Long Lonely Winter

The trees are bare, the snow falls down
I'm locked in bed, safe and sound
The deafening silence, rings in my ears
One day soon you'll be near
The suns gone down four years before
There's been so much to keep me sore
The clock ticks slowly on the wall
I think of days before the fall
How can one love, fill me with fear
Keep your distance, don't get too near
A world of sorrow, and discontent
Starving children, war mongers hell bent
But still I sit here in my chair
I've changed my ways, I've cut my hair
But inside no feelings, but I'll stay alive
Waiting for spring to arrive.

Once

Why do we do this, when we don't enjoy,
Letting the rich man use you as a toy? One day, Oh! one day, all this
will change!
Just give me some time and I'll rearrange.
Why do we let them dictate when they're wrong?
I wish it would change,
The same thing for too long.
Stuck in a rut, hear the screams and the shouts,
Knowing inside, it is time to get out.
Everyday go to work, say the same old things,
There's no heart inside you, you can't even sing.
One day, Oh! one day, when it's all been said,
You're old and burned out, then you are dead.
Why do we sit here and take all the flack?
Get yourself up, it's time to attack!
Because when you're gone, no one will care.
Life should be wondrous, life should be fair.
One day, Oh! one day, when I look to the sky,
I'll get out of this, forever Good-bye.
And I'll tell my children, do what they will,
Because life is a waste, when you're not fulfilled.

Hello

My head down so long, but I don't count the days
Seeing the light at the end of the maze
Now she is waiting, with her white dress on
My head is singing, a new age has dawned
I've been in the gutter, for forever it seems
The turmoil I've been put through, the suffering I've seen
On the road to destruction, with self abuse
I'd tell you my story, but what's the use?
Everyone has their problems, but it's so hard to see
I worry too much, about what's happening to me
If this is my life and my destiny
At the end of this pain, I'll be set free
What's on the other side, is there a God?
I wish he'd help me, for I feel like a dog.
Was there a Jesus high up on the cross?
So much war and killing, all because of his cost
I've been down in hell, now I have returned
When I see her standing, my stomach it churns
There are many answers I need to know
I stand in the corner, then she says hello.
My mind goes a blank, I'm frozen with fear
I can't move an inch, when she comes near.
Take me in your arms, erase these bad thoughts
You are the one, all my life I've sought.

The Fruit

You are like an Apple, so juicy and ripe
I want to eat you, all day and all night.
Your body so wondrous, Oh! what a sight.
I need you forever, for you are the light.
Your breasts are like pears, with cherries on top,
When you slide off our clothes, I like what you've got.
Your eyes are like crystals, a sparkling blue,
I am so happy, now I have found you.
You are an Angel, sent down to save,
I'll be your servant, let me be your slave,
Forever I'm yours, I won't let you down,
Your limbs wrapped around me, now we are earthbound.
You are my saviour, you are my pan,
You are the reason, I am who I am.
Before I was nervous, locked in this world's strife,
Then you walked right in, and I saw the life.
Your lips are like strawberries, a voluptuous red.
You're my warmth in the night when lying in bed.
The roots of my life, you've come to sow,
Get my head held up high, and out of self wallow.
You are like a peach, your velvet smooth thighs,
What would I do, if you said goodbye?

Janine

On a Midsummer's Night, down at Glastonbury
Through a multitude of people I could see
An Angelic girl with a candle in hand
Knowing she's to be the one, for the Promise Land.
Dressed in a Kaftan, her hair long and white,
She lifted my gloom, and brought back delight.
I told her my troubles, apologetically.
She said don't be silly, she really liked me.
Walking for hours, seeing all the side shows,
Where is she now, God only knows.
I asked her, her name, she replied Janine,
A smile on her face, like a laser beam,
I wanted to love her, that very night,
But losing her company, put me in fright.
So we walked forever, then she said Farewell,
I'll see you tomorrow, but you can never tell,
Now she is gone, it was all in such haste,
If we meet again, it will be our fate.
Lost in the fields, the emptiness is back,
I'll see her again, and that is a fact.
She is the best one I've met or seen.
I hope you can feel me, I love you Janine.

The Good Days

She's wondrous, like the brightest stars
Whether she is near or far.
No need to hang out in sleazy bars
I've got her to take me to Mars.
She makes me laugh, when I feel down,
Always smiling never a frown
Like Siamese twins we are bound -
I'm so glad, that I have found,
Her eyes like whirlpools a sparkling blue.
We'll lie naked in the morning dew
I know her well, she loves me too,
The things I wanted, but never knew
She smells so nice, like a garden of roses
Unlike the others no threat she poses
I'll stay with her until she dozes
She makes me feel as strong as Moses
My love for her will never fade
She shone her light on to my shade
Everyone said it was forbade
But we both knew, we had it made.

In Love

It's time for my sleep, and I'm lying here
I wish for your touch just to feel you near
You are in my soul, you are in my dreams
Sometimes life is easier than it probably seems
I look to the sky, I need you tonight
Forever and ever, for you are so right
Can you feel the power, whenever we meet?
After I walk off, as if I owned the street
My love, come with me, for you understand
I melt right away, with the touch of your hand.

The Blues

When you find out who you are, you will find me in the bar
Drinking with my so called friends -
They all vanish, when the money ends.
When you find out it's for real you'll find me lying in a field
Lost in a world of broken dreams
There is no time left to redream.
Our love has gone, it just wore out
Everyday, we scream and shout
Now I'm up to my neck in drink
Just three more, and I won't think.
But everyone's had their fair share
Why on earth should they care?
When the yes turns to a no
I will know it's time to go.
Our nerves are crumbling, row by row
The candles we lit, we have to blow
You will find me in a glass
Just three more and, it will pass.

Ah!

Make love to me, the sweetest girl
Make love to me, give me my fill!
Make love to me, as if it's your last,
Forget the worry of the past.
Make sweetest love, we are as one,
Make sweetest love, and watch the sun.
Too long it's been, since I've been loved,
Too long it's been my gentle dove.

Black Clouds

The logs burn brightly upon the fire
I look to the skies and fill with desire
Looking around, but no one is near Oh! how I wish she was still here
The trees and the bushes, move freely in the wind.
A warmth, fills my soul, a glow from within
I've searched high and low, but still I can't find
The woman in black, who I've been unkind
Here she comes now she walks, with the flow
Here she comes now she is in the know
The fire goes down, I look to the moon
Anticipating, she will be back soon
She'll wrap her arms around me, it's so hard to forgive
But without her touch, I just can't live
Here she comes now Angelic and free
Here she comes now she's smiling at me
The logs burn brightly, the moon's gone away
Erasing the past, for this is today.

Dumbstruck

I'm so frightened lady,
Frightened of your smile.
My soul's destroyed, so I can't talk,
So I'll just run for miles.
Take me to your darkest thoughts,
Let me feel your heart.
If you kiss me with sweet lips, it will be a start.
I'm so frightened woman, because I think you're all right,
But every time I go to talk my mouth locks up in fright,
So take me to your sweetest dreams,
Let me feel your sun,
Let me be your tower of strength,
For you're the only one.

Where?

Now where has all the music gone?
Whatever happened to our songs?
Now the vital spark's gone out
Inside my head they scream and shout.
Whatever happened to warming smiles?
My feet are sore, I've walked for miles
Wondering where we went wrong.
The disappearance of our song.
But life goes on, a new beginning
Soon someone new will be singing
And 'us' won't matter anymore
But once my sweet thing I adored.

All My Life

Breaking the silence, she whispers sweetly
My heart is racing wild
All my life, searched for story
Now I have found that child
Her snake-like eyes, the hypnotic stare
Sending me to heaven
A girl so free, so life, so fair
She is lucky seven
The sun goes down, the sky turns red, the nightly chill sets in
Her legs wrap round my neck and head, her warmth comes from
within.
All my life, I've searched for her, now my vocation's complete
Walking as if ten feet tall, now I am the élite
Breaking the silence of the night, I kiss her cherry lips
Then from the blood filled golden cup, our love juice we do sip.

I Love You

I love you, my gentle one
I love you, you are my sun.
I want you forever more
Can't you see, that I adore

I'll be yours when you feel down
I'll make you laugh, I'll be your clown
I'll wipe away your tears and pain
I'll make you warm, when there is rain

I love you, don't run away
I love you, please, won't you stay
I feel for you, deep down inside
If you feel low, you can confide.

Insanity

The moon's fallen down
To the soft mossy ground
The sky has gone out
It's jump up and shout
The stars have come up
Grab your spoon and your cup
Fill to the brim, altogether we'll sup
The sun has gone down
For the monkey and clown
So grab your spoon, and gobble it down
Dance round a square, shave off your hair
Make love to the moon
For the monkey is doomed.

The Anticipation

I'm wild with desire, for a love, strong and pure
For my days are numbered, getting fewer and fewer
Where are you hiding? Please come out of your shell
They say it will happen, but how can I tell?
I'm fired up with passion, just waiting to smother
I want a woman, to hold me and mother
A girl who will stand by, when I go off the rails
Not giving me tests, that I'm sure to fail
I've seen her standing, but I'm frightened to talk
Staring all night, hypnotised by her walk
Thinking too much, as another steps in
Knowing inside, I'm much better than him
I'm exploding inside, like a raging fire
My soul feels so empty, life's looking dire
I hope one day soon, I wish it today
She'll walk through the door, and whisk me away
I'm full of confusion, not knowing what I want
But if I get you, I'll have the lot.

Regrets

When you're eighty years old all wrinkled and grey
I would still want you like I do today
When the years have passed by, and there's no need to be blue
I hope you'll still smile the way that you do
When your joints are stiff and you trudge across the floor
I would still love you, I'd still adore
I want you girl, like I've never wanted
Your spirit is in me, your eyes have taunted
When you're old and wasted, and you're all alone
I hope you don't regret, the day you slammed down the phone
We have one short life, I want mine with you
So hold me and love me, for my love is true.

Obvious

Drink to oblivion, for the ego that hurts
Dance on the table and rip off your shirt
Only twelve hours to live, so I might as well sin
Goodbye sweet one, tell my next of kin
Drink till you drop, for who really cares
About clothes on your back or the length of your hair?
My life is over, and I was so free
You might say I faked, but it really was me
Goodbye green trees and mountains so high
When I felt down, you made me sigh
You gave me meaning to trundle along
You made me know, I did belong
Hello sweet heaven, I've been here before
Remember the last one, that I adored
But it was in vain, for she loved another
Now she's dressed in black, and she has discovered.

The Sea of ABYSS

Lost to the world, in the sea of Abyss.
Once down in the gutter, now this life is bliss,
Since I have found you, my vocation's complete
I've reached the heights, to become the élite
A new found confidence, I'm so self assured
She is my love, like the water so pure
I'll never leave her, smitten with lust
I've found the one to hold and to trust
Whenever I see her, the blood starts to flow
She makes me happy, once I felt so low
Life is so beautiful, with her in my world
If I'm in heaven, I thank you my girl
The moon shines down on you, the stars are array
I look up and smile, for this is my day
You are so precious, like nothing before
My head's come together, it's you I adore
I stare at the flowers, I laugh with the trees
I feel so lucky, I was born to be me.

Where has Love Gone?

The love flows like a stream, from a heart that is true
I want to be near you and do what you do
Where on this earth, could there be such a sight
She leaves in the morning and creeps in the night
Rolling embraced, as one for an hour
A need that's so great, it's sure to devour.
Change my wanton ways, but that's how we met
Enquiring her inner thoughts, you've become a threat
The jealousy twists, a wrenching inside
Lying on the sand, waiting for the next tide
In a puff of smoke, she left as she came
Her mission complete, now she has tamed
The rain and the wind, from the crack on the ceiling
Whistles and pours, but still there's no feeling
The guilt and the anger, humiliation and pain
There will be another, but it's such a shame
She came in the night, trailing fragrance of incense
Try to ignore, but her eyes so intense
Now she has vanished, was it all in a dream?
The need to go on, has disappeared so it seems.

Fateful Yours

Dry your eyes my sweet child and we'll walk
To the sky my sweet love, let us talk
Everything is all right, everything is okay
Rest your troubled mind, forget yesterday.

He's a bad one I know, but it's over
Broke your heart, gentle one, he's a rover
But he's gone, and my heart aches for you
Put a smile on your face, don't be blue
I love you with my mind, with my soul
Take my hand, pretty one, let us stroll
What may come, what may go, I'll be yours
Kiss my lips, gorgeous one, you're so pure.

Dry your eyes, sweetest one, and we'll walk
Through the fields of love, and we'll talk.

Dead End Street

I wish you could see, I'd give you my world
I'd change my ideas just for you girl
I'd sail the seven seas, I'd climb mountains high
My honour is true, I'd give you no lies
I wish I could watch you, asleep at night
Safe in your bedroom, no sound or sight
Is it all in vain, me spilling my heart
I'd say what I feel
But where would I start?
I wish you knew, these feelings of mine
Outside I seem confident, but inside I pine
For your sweet love, I'd change my bad ways
But you're spoken for, and I'm left in a maze.